# VIRGINIA WOOLF

# Nurse Lugton's Curtain

## ILLUSTRATED BY
## JULIE VIVAS

GULLIVER BOOKS • HARCOURT, INC.

*Orlando   Austin   New York   San Diego   Toronto   London*

*Printed in Singapore*

Nurse Lugton was asleep. She had given one great snore. She had dropped her head; thrust her spectacles up her forehead; and there she sat by the fender with her finger sticking up and a thimble on it; and her needle full of cotton hanging down; and she was snoring, snoring; and on her knees, covering the whole of her apron, was a large piece of figured blue stuff.

The animals with which it was covered did not move till Nurse Lugton snored for the fifth time. One, two, three, four, five—ah, the old woman was at last asleep. The antelope nodded to the zebra; the giraffe bit through the leaf on the tree top; all the animals began to toss and prance.

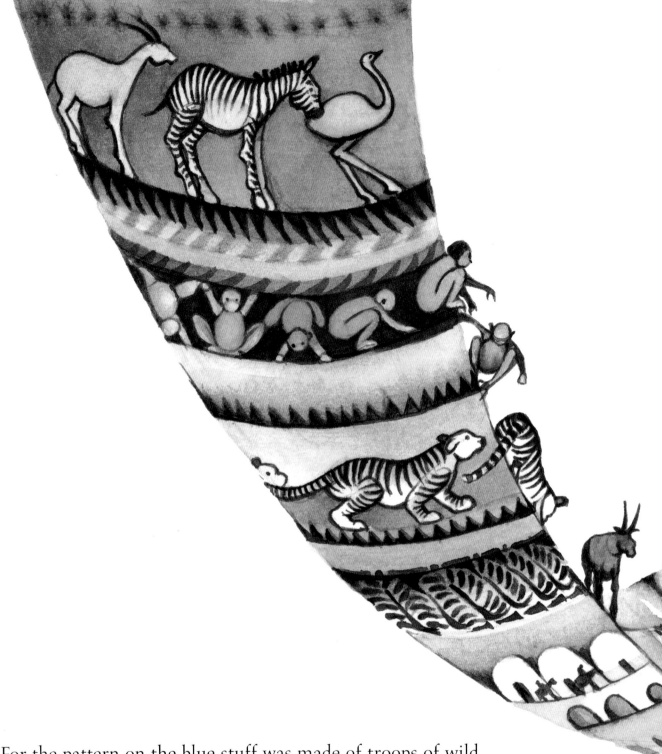

For the pattern on the blue stuff was made of troops of wild beasts and below them was a lake and a bridge and a town with round roofs and little men and women looking out of the windows and riding over the bridge on horseback.

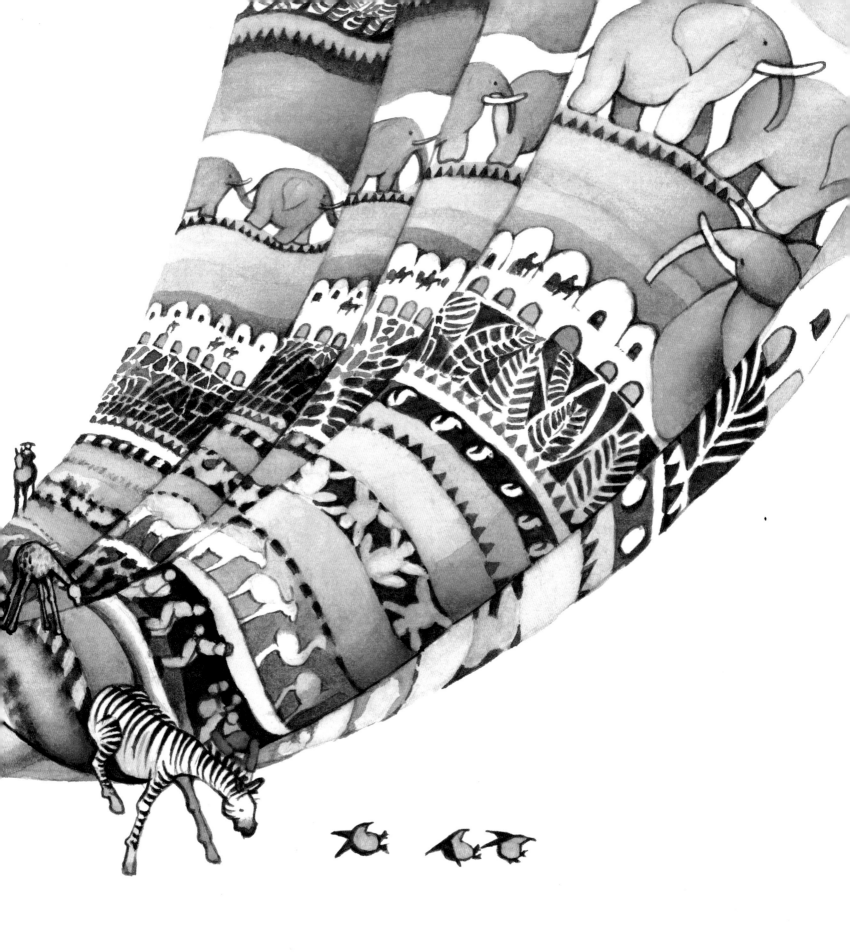

But directly the old nurse snored for the fifth time,
the blue stuff turned to blue air; the trees waved;
you could hear the water of the lake breaking; and
see the people moving over the bridge and waving
their hands out of the windows.

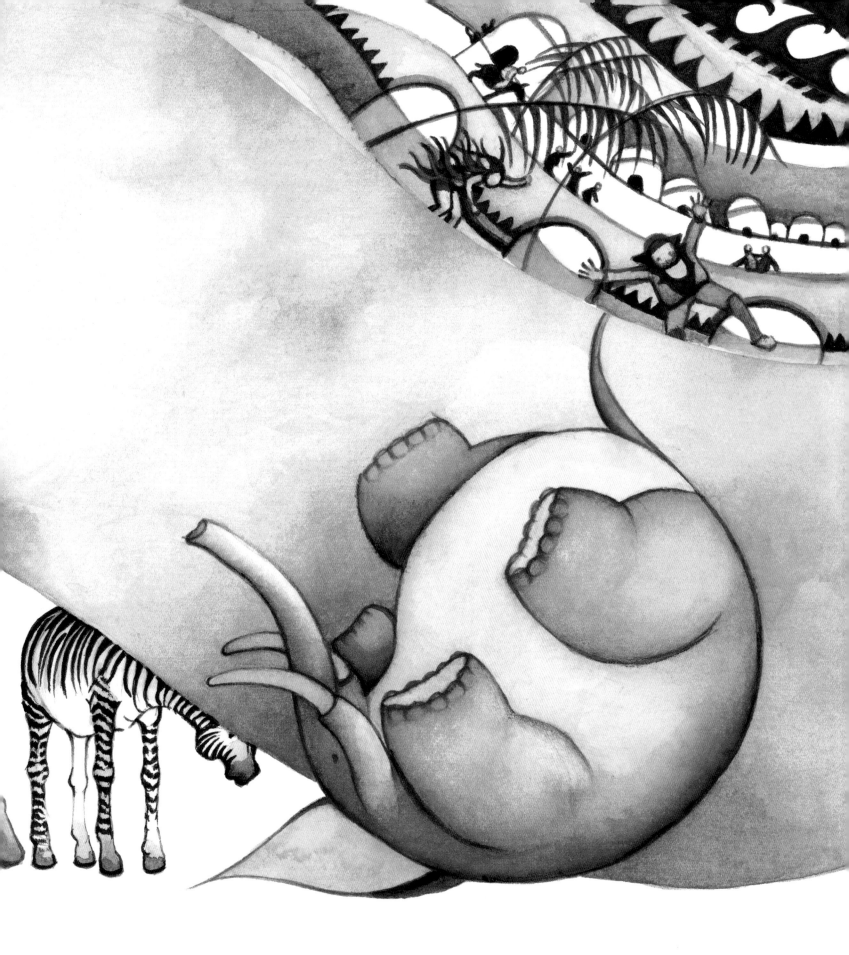

The animals now began to move. First went the elephant and the zebra; next the giraffe and the tiger; the ostrich, the mandrill, twelve marmots and a pack of mongeese followed; the penguins and the pelicans waddled and waded, often pecking at each other, alongside.

Over them burnt Nurse Lugton's golden thimble like a sun; and as Nurse Lugton snored, the animals heard the wind roaring through the forest. Down they went to drink, and as they trod, the blue curtain (for Nurse Lugton was making a curtain for Mrs. John Jasper Gingham's drawing-room window) became made of grass, and roses and daisies; strewn with white and black stones; with puddles on it, and cart tracks, and little frogs hopping quickly lest the elephants should tread on them. Down they went, down the hill to the lake to drink.

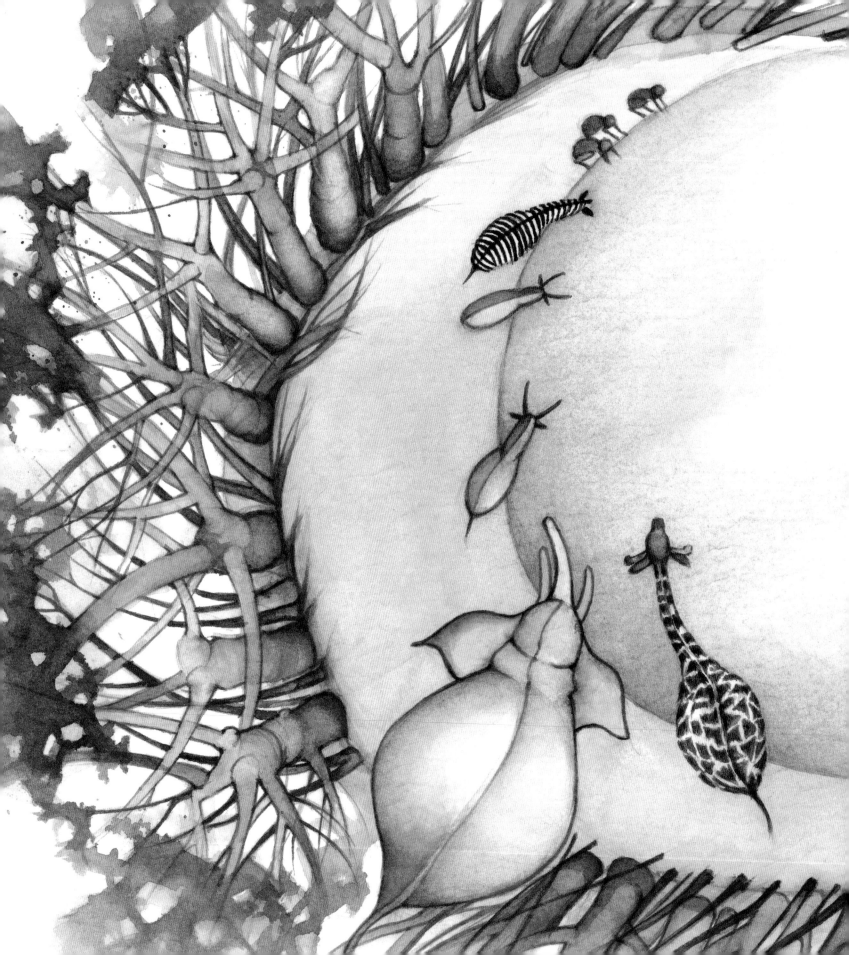

And soon all were gathered on the edge of the lake,
some stooping down, others throwing their heads up.
Really, it was a beautiful sight—

and to think of all this lying across old Nurse Lugton's knees while she slept, sitting on her Windsor chair in the lamplight—to think of her apron covered with roses and grass, and with all these wild beasts trampling on it, when Nurse Lugton was mortally afraid even of poking through the bars with her umbrella at the Zoo! Even a little black beetle made her jump. But Nurse Lugton slept; Nurse Lugton saw nothing at all.

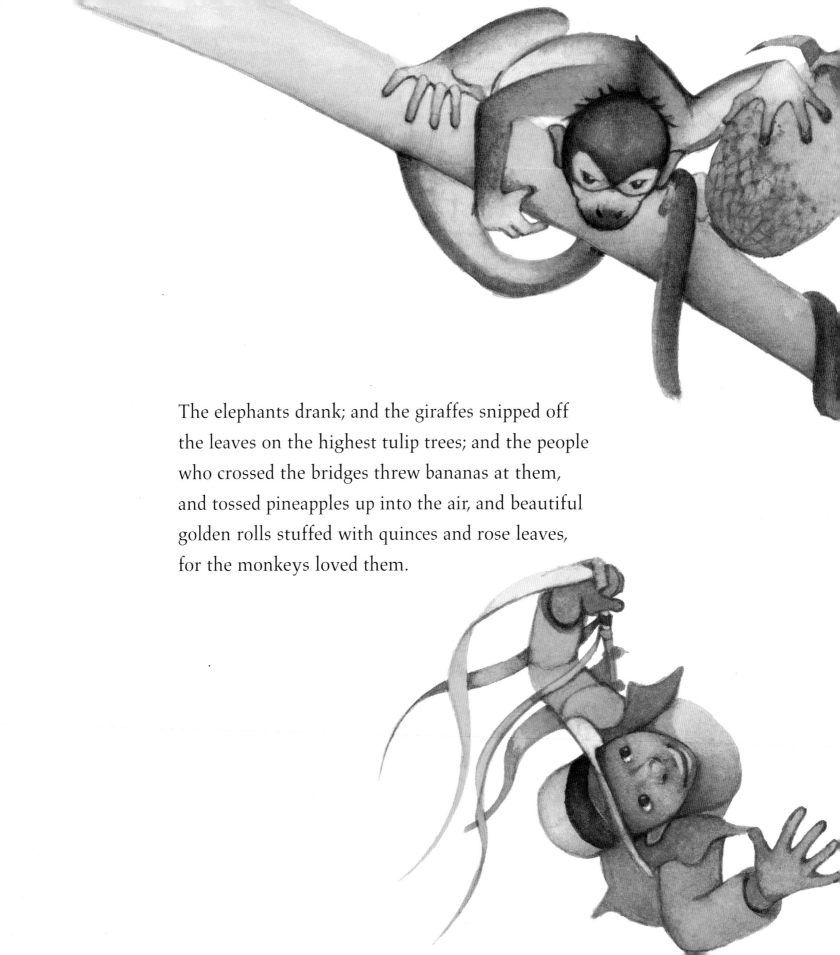

The elephants drank; and the giraffes snipped off
the leaves on the highest tulip trees; and the people
who crossed the bridges threw bananas at them,
and tossed pineapples up into the air, and beautiful
golden rolls stuffed with quinces and rose leaves,
for the monkeys loved them.

The old Queen came by in her palanquin; the general of the army passed; so did the Prime Minister; the Admiral, the Executioner; and great dignitaries on business in the town, which was a very beautiful place called Millamarchmantopolis.

Nobody harmed the lovely beasts; many pitied them; for it was well known that even the smallest monkey was enchanted. For a great ogress had them in her toils, the people knew; and the great ogress was called Lugton.

They could see her, from their windows, towering over them. She had a face like the side of a mountain with great precipices and avalanches, and chasms for her eyes and hair and nose and teeth. And every animal which strayed into her territories she froze alive, so that all day they stood stock still on her knee, but when she fell asleep, then they were released, and down they came in the evening to Millamarchmantopolis to drink.

Suddenly old Nurse Lugton twitched the curtain all in crinkles.
For a big bluebottle was buzzing round the lamp, and woke her.
Up she sat and stuck her needle in.

The animals flashed back in a second.
The air became blue stuff.

And the curtain lay quite still on her knee. Nurse Lugton took up her needle, and went on sewing Mrs. Gingham's drawing-room curtain.

*The story of Nurse Lugton and her magical curtain was first found among the pages of Virginia Woolf's manuscript for her novel* Mrs. Dalloway. *It was probably written in the fall of 1924 but was not actually published until 1965, when the story was included in a collection. Leonard Woolf said that his wife wrote the story for her niece Ann Stephen, when the child was visiting her aunt in the English countryside.*

First published 1991
Redesigned edition 2004

The Library of Congress has cataloged an earlier edition as follows:
Woolf, Virginia, 1882–1941.
Nurse Lugton's curtain/written by Virginia Woolf; illustrated by Julie Vivas.
p. cm.
"Gulliver Books."
Summary: As Nurse Lugton dozes, the animals on the patterned curtain she is sewing come alive.
[1. Animals—Fiction. 2. Fantasy.]
I. Vivas, Julie, 1947– ill. II. Title.
PZ7.W88155Nu 1991
[E]—dc20 90-5087
ISBN 0-15-205048-5

A C E G H F D B

The display type was hand lettered by Georgia Deaver.
The text type was set in Aldus Roman.
Color separations by Bright Arts Ltd., Hong Kong
Printed and bound by Tien Wah Press, Singapore
This book was printed on totally chlorine-free Stora Enso Matte paper.
Production supervision by Sandra Grebenar and Ginger Boyer
Designed by Judythe Sieck